Enid Blyton's
NODDY
and the Naughty Tail

BBC BOOKS

It was going to be another busy day for Noddy. "I must have a big breakfast," he thought. "It will give me lots of strength."

Just as he was finishing his last piece of toast, there was a loud knock on his door.

"That sounds like Bert Monkey," thought Noddy. "I'll need lots of strength to deal with him."

"I need your help, Noddy," said Bert, as his
tail swished the lid from Noddy's teapot.
    "You can help *me* by looking
after your tail," said Noddy,
crossly.

Bert explained that his grandma had given him a pencil box. "But it hadn't got a rubber, and I really wanted one," he said. His tail sneaked out and grabbed Noddy's toast.

"I want that toast!" cried Noddy. Bert's tail put it back.

"It was my tail that found me a rubber," said
Bert. "It was from my grandma's. It's really
big, and it can rub out *anything*."

"Then don't bring it in here!" said Noddy in
alarm. "You must give it back."

"I can't," said Bert Monkey. "I've sold the
pencil box to Sam Skittle."

"That rubber is dangerous," said Noddy. "We must find Sam."

Meanwhile, Bert's naughty tail was trying to take his hat *and* Noddy's marmalade!

"Put my marmalade back, please," said
Noddy, and the tail obeyed.

Bert explained that the Skittles were off to
the seaside, by train, that very day.

"We must hurry and catch them," he said.

The Skittle family arrived at the station just as Noddy's car appeared. But Bert Monkey's tail squirmed right across Noddy's eyes.

"I can't see!" he cried. The car bumped gently into Sally Skittle, and one by one all the Skittles fell over.

The Skittle family giggled. They loved being knocked over.

"Thanks, Noddy," said Sam Skittle. "That was fun. How's your tail?" he asked Bert Monkey. Bert's tail shook Sam's hand. Everyone laughed.

"I need that pencil box," said Bert Monkey.
"I'll give you back your money, Sam."
"Here's the pencil box," said Sam.
"But I've given the rubber to the
Clockwork Mouse."

"We must go to the market,"
said Noddy. "That's where
he'll be."

The market was busy. And there was the Clockwork Mouse. Suddenly Bert Monkey's tail tapped him on the shoulder.

"Have you got the rubber Sam Skittle gave you?" asked Noddy.

The Clockwork Mouse jumped.

"I might, or I might not have it," he said, unhelpfully. "Give me a free ride in your car, Noddy," he added, "and I might give you the rubber then."

"Oh, very well!" said Noddy, and the Clockwork Mouse climbed into the car.

They drove out of Toy Town and into the
countryside. The Clockwork Mouse was
enjoying himself. Back in Toy Town again
Noddy's car very nearly ran into Mr Plod.
He shook his fist angrily at Noddy as the
car raced past.

At the end of the ride, Noddy asked for the rubber.

"I haven't got it," said the Clockwork Mouse. "It kept falling through holes in my pockets. Bumpy Dog ran off with it."

"Oh, no," said Noddy. "We'll have to find him now. Come on, Bert."

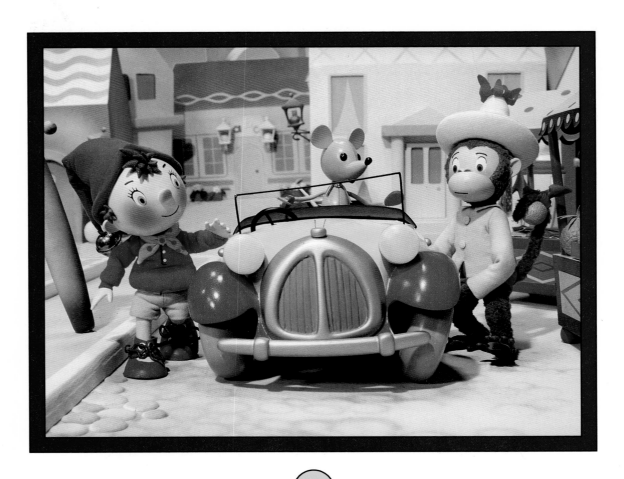

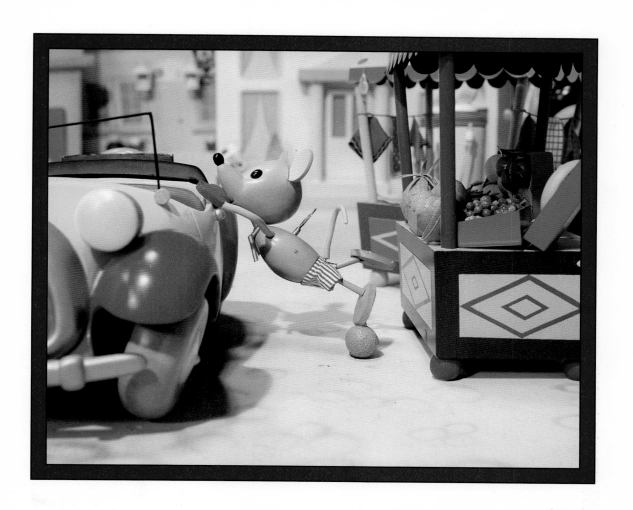

Noddy and Bert Monkey set off to find Bumpy Dog. The Clockwork Mouse laughed at Bert Monkey's tail. The tail suddenly bowled an orange at him and tripped him up. The Clockwork Mouse squeaked with surprise.

"Have you seen Tessie Bear and Bumpy Dog?" Noddy asked Dinah Doll. "I think they've gone to the café for ice-creams," she said. As she spoke, Bert's tail picked up an ornament from her stall, but Dinah Doll soon took it back.

Noddy and Bert Monkey arrived at the café.
They looked worried.

"Where's Bumpy Dog?" said Noddy,
anxiously.

"He's at my house," said Mrs Tubby Bear.
"When I left he and Master Tubby were
throwing a rubber about."

"That's Bert's rubber," said Noddy. "He needs it. Thank you, Mrs Tubby Bear."

Meanwhile Bert Monkey's tail was trying to give Mrs Tubby's ice-cream to Bert!

But Bert didn't have time to stop. He hurried after Noddy.

"I do hope Bumpy Dog is still here,"
said Noddy, as they came to the Tubby
Bears' house.

    "Woof, woof!" He heard Bumpy bark.
Noddy walked straight into the
door, expecting it to open.

    "Ow!" he said. It was stuck fast.

Bert and Noddy peered through the window. Bumpy Dog had knocked over a chair. It was blocking the front door.

"Look," exclaimed Bert. "Master Tubby's making holes everywhere with my magic rubber!"

"We must get it back, Bert," said Noddy.
"Tubby," he shouted, "stop using that rubber!"

Master Tubby Bear shook his head. "I won't,"
he said. "I like it. It's mine. Bumpy Dog gave it
to me."

"But he didn't know it was *magic*!" explained Noddy.

"Oooh," said Tubby. "Is it really magic?"

He rubbed a hole in a cushion.

"Stop it!" shouted Noddy. "Try to grab that rubber!" he called to Bumpy Dog.

But Bumpy Dog only made things worse. He jumped about, bumping into furniture and sending ornaments flying.

"Go away," said Master Tubby Bear, "or I'll rub you out, Bumpy Dog!"

Then Master Tubby started to rub out the
chair by the front door. Soon it had
disappeared completely.

"Come on, Bert," said Noddy. "We can get
in now!"

And they rushed through the door.

Bert's tail wrapped around the rubber.

"That's my rubber. You must give it to me," Bert Monkey said to Master Tubby Bear.

"No," said Tubby Bear sulkily. "Shan't." He began to rub out the tip of Bert's tail.

Noddy was pleased that Bert's tail could be
rubbed out. But Bert wasn't.
   "My tail!" he wailed.
      "You shan't have my magic rubber,"
      said Master Tubby Bear. He stepped
      backwards, fell over Bumpy Dog,
      and dropped the rubber!

Noddy picked it up quickly.

"At last," he said, triumphantly. "Now, Master Tubby. What shall I rub out first – your nose, or your mouth?"

"No, no!" shrieked Master Tubby Bear. "Leave me alone, Noddy!" He ran out of the door.

Bert Monkey sat down on a chair. He was exhausted.

"Thank you, Noddy," he said. "I'm so glad we found that rubber."

But can you guess what Noddy was doing? He was quickly rubbing out the rest of Bert Monkey's tail!

"You have a rest, Bert" said Noddy. "I'll tidy up. I don't know what Mrs Tubby Bear will say about all these holes!"

By now, Bert's tail had disappeared.

"I know," exclaimed Bert, "I'll ask my grandma for a come-back spell!"

"Be quick," said Noddy. "And don't let that tail slow you down, Bert," he added with a grin.

"I won't," replied Bert Monkey. "Haven't you noticed, Noddy? My tail is suddenly being very good indeed!"

Noddy laughed as Bumpy Dog jumped
about happily.

"I'm pleased I had that extra piece of toast,
Bumpy. It made me strong enough to sort out
all that excitement!"

Other Noddy *TV Tie-in titles*
available from BBC Children's Books

Noddy and his Bell
Noddy and the Goblins
Noddy Loses Sixpence
Noddy and Martha Monkey
Noddy and his New Friend
Noddy and the Kite
Noddy and the Pouring Rain

Other TV Tie-in titles in preparation

Noddy and the Broken Bicycle
Noddy Delivers Some Parcels
Noddy Gets a New Job
Noddy and the Milkman
Noddy and the Special Key

Published by BBC Books
a division of BBC Enterprises Limited
Woodlands, 80 Wood Lane, London W12 0TT
First published 1992
Reprinted 1992
Text and stills copyright © BBC Enterprises Limited 1992
ISBN 0 563 36854 3

Based on the Television series, produced by
Cosgrove Hall Productions, inspired by the Noddy Books
which are copyright Darrell Waters Limited 1949-1968

Enid Blyton's signature and Noddy are Trademarks of Darrell Waters Limited

Designed and typeset in 17/21pt Garamond by Between the Lines, London

Printed and bound in Great Britain by Cambus Limited, East Kilbride
Colour separations by DOT Gradations, Chelmsford
Cover printed by Cambus Limited, East Kilbride